LULU
THE LLAMACORN

written by ROSINA MIRABELLA • illustrated by MORGAN HUFF

HARPER
An Imprint of HarperCollinsPublishers

Lulu is a llamacorn.

Which means she's half llama, half unicorn, and 100 percent magic.

Some would say she's a *gllamacorn* since Lulu was the most glamorous creature in all of Magic Meadows.

Her father, Harold, had wings that let him soar through the stars.

Her mother, Credenza, had a dashing smile of powerful pearly teeth.

Lulu had *both*.
But what truly set Lulu apart was her perfectly fluffy tail.

There was no doubt that Lulu was the most dazzling, the most impressive, the most—WAIT.
Lulu wiped her fancy glasses to get a better look at what was in front of her . . .

"That Pegasus has bigger wings than me!"

This just couldn't be. How could Lulu be the most glam if she didn't have the biggest wings? Would she even be glam at all?

Luckily, Lulu had a plan.

Lulu called Karen the Flower Fairy.
Karen didn't care very much about
glamour, but she cared about Lulu.
She was Lulu's best and cleverest
friend by far!

"I thought I had the biggest, most
beautiful wings in all the world, but
I don't think that's true anymore.
Can you help me get bigger wings?
Please, please, please?" Lulu asked.

"Well, if it's important to you, all right," Karen replied.
"No *probllama!*"
She flicked her wand one, two, three times in a circle.

"Perfection." Lulu beamed.
Lulu was the most glam once again.
Or so she thought.
Before she spotted something shiny over by the Waterfall of Wonders . . .

"Oh gee! That mermaid has the shiniest, brightest tail I have ever seen.

"If I am to be as glam as her, I just have to have a shiny tail, too. Then I will truly sparkle with joy!"

"I do want you to be happy," Karen said as she picked up her wand again.

But before Karen could finish, Lulu perked up.

"KAREN—do you see the
TEETH on that dragon?

Having those would make me smile
big smiles forever and ever."

"What a *dramacorn*," Karen thought as she sighed, flicked her wand, and granted Lulu's wishes.

The next day, the new and improved Lulu pranced to the neighborhood picnic feeling on top of the world. Until . . .

She didn't.

"Excuse me."

"Whoops."

"Pardon me."

"Oh, Grandma,
I'm so sorry!"

"Maybe these wings are *too big*" thought Lulu,
but she quickly put it out of her mind. She would get her
chance to really SHINE at the sky basketball game that
afternoon. That would go much better.

But it was worse.

"Ahh, my eye!"

Her tail blinded all the players and Coach Cyclops, too.

Lulu was disappointed. Nothing seemed to be going right.

"Basketball, smasketball," said Karen. "Let's watch a movie and eat popcorn instead. Your brand-new choppers are perfect for it!"

Lulu soon found out that they weren't.

CRUNCH.

MUNCH.

OUCH!

Lulu didn't feel glam or sparkly and couldn't even smile a big smile.

"Karen, being this glamorous is ruining *everything*," Lulu cried.

"You know, I always thought you were perfectly glamorous just the way you were," Karen said.

Lulu sniffed. She thought Karen might be on to something.

"Well, my wings did fly me around just fine. . . .

"I did like going to the hairdresser to get my tail groomed. . . .

"And it was so easy to smile. I smiled all the time. Just being myself.
"Maybe that was what really made me so glam!"

Karen sniffed back. "Precisely! Besides, do you think I'd call anyone my best friend who wasn't glamorous inside out and all on their own? I'm a fairy, Lulu. I have standards."

Karen had a point.
With an approving nod from Lulu,
Karen flicked her wand one last time.

Lulu was half llama, half unicorn, and 100 percent herself.
And that made Lulu very happy.

HARPER
An Imprint of HarperCollinsPublishers   www.harpercollinschildrens.com   Illustrations © 2020 by Morgan Huff

HARPER
An Imprint of HarperCollinsPublishers   www.harpercollinschildrens.com   Illustrations © 2020 by Morgan Huff